ENTICINGLY ECCENTRIC
GNOMES

ENTICINGLY ECCENTRIC
GNOMES

Create your own enchanting, naughty gnomes

Bath · New York · Singapore · Hong Kong · Cologne · Delhi
Melbourne · Amsterdam · Johannesburg · Auckland · Shenzhen

This edition published by Parragon Books Ltd
in 2013 and distributed by

Parragon Inc.
440 Park Avenue South, 13th Floor
New York, NY 10016
www.parragon.com

Designed by Pink Creative
Illustrations by Ummagumma
Project managed by Frances Prior-Reeves

ISBN 978-1-4454-8865-3

Printed in China

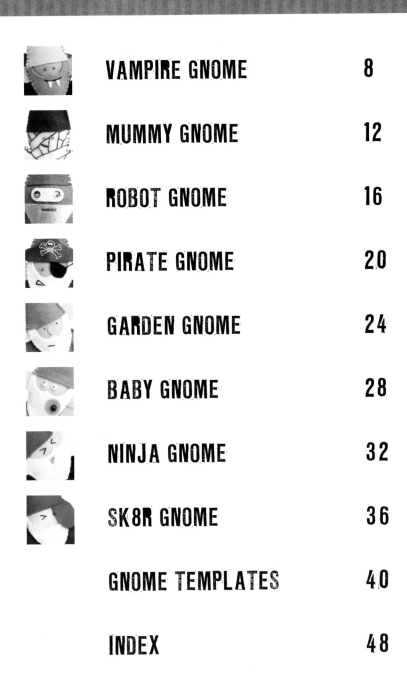

ENTICINGLY ECCENTRIC
GNOMES

Some gnomes are here to steal all of the belongings from your backyard (and perhaps from your house, too!), piece by piece, but never fear: there are some gnomes who have made it their sole purpose to protect your earthly treasures. Even those committed to protecting you could turn out to be more irritating than you'd anticipated though, so watch out.

Either way, these little creatures are here to brighten up your day—maybe you'll want to make a couple for your friends to adopt for a special occasion. All you need to create each gnome is listed at the start of the instructions. For all projects you'll need scissors and an embroidery needle. You might also find pins helpful to attach your paper templates to the fabric before cutting. All the templates you will need are included in the back, ready for you to copy them, cut them out, and start creating your own gnome family.

If you want to start with an easier project try Baby Gnome (p.28)—he's simple to make, cute, cuddly, and ready to play. The other gnomes will be fighting for your affections to get you to make them. For a slightly more complex project, try Garden Gnome (p.24)—he's gentle, kind, and will protect your personal kingdom from mischievous characters, such as Sk8r Gnome (p.36).

MAKING "VAMPIRE GNOME"

1 Photocopy or trace all the templates on page 40. Cut the BEARD from gray felt and the FACE from beige felt. Glue the BEARD to the FACE.

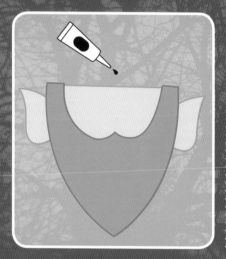

2 Cut the HAT from pale blue felt and glue the bottom edge to the top edge of the FACE. Sew the two small beads to the FACE using red floss.

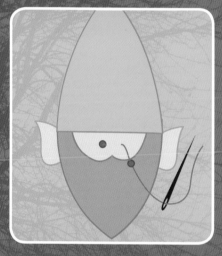

MATERIALS

Gray felt, beige felt, pale blue felt, white felt, black felt, brown felt, green felt, red felt

Red, black, and gray stranded embroidery floss

2 small red beads

Pins, Craft glue, Toy fiberfill

Embroidery needle, Scissors

Templates from page 40

VAMPIRE GNOME

Scaring local wildlife and glimmering with murderous intent, this gnome prowls around alone at night. But he just wants a friend and wishes that he was *gnormal*.

3 Sew a mouth onto the BEARD using black floss. Cut the two TEETH from white felt and glue them onto the BEARD, touching the mouth.

4 Cut the HEAD BACK from beige felt and sew to the back of the completed head using gray floss. Leave a small opening. Stuff the head with fiberfill and then close the opening.

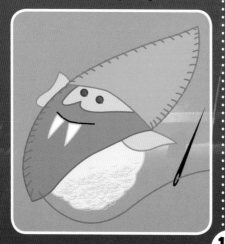

5 Cut the BODY from black felt and the BOOTS from brown felt. Glue the BOOTS to the bottom of the BODY.

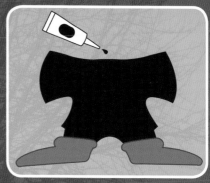

6 Cut the BODY BACK from red felt and the HANDS from beige felt. Glue the HANDS in place.

7 Sew the BODY BACK to the back of the BODY using red floss. Leave a small opening.

8 Stuff the BODY with a small amount of fiberfill, then close the opening.

9 Cut the BELT from green felt and glue to the BODY. Cut the BUCKLE from pale blue felt and glue to the BELT.

10 Sew the head to the BODY along the top of the BODY using red floss.

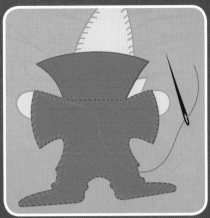

11 Lift up the BEARD and dab a small amount of glue to fix the BEARD to the BODY.

FANG-TASTIC!

MUMMY GNOME

The oldest of the gnomes, he's seen every trick in the book... and he's got a few more up his unraveling sleeve!

MATERIALS

White felt, dark green felt, brown felt, blue felt, light green felt

Black, brown, and green stranded embroidery floss

2 small green beads

Pins, Craft glue, Toy fiberfill

Embroidery needle

Scissors

Templates from page 41

MAKING "MUMMY GNOME"

1 Photocopy or trace all the templates on page 41. Cut the BODY from white felt. Using brown floss, embroider the bandage details...so it looks like this.

2 Using green floss, sew on the two green beads for the eyes.

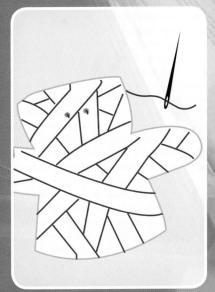

3 Using black floss, sew in the mouth.

5 Cut the PANTS from dark green felt and glue them to the bottom edge of the BODY.

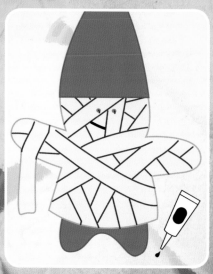

WHAT`S INSIDE?

4 Cut the HAT from dark green felt and glue the bottom edge to the top edge of the BODY.

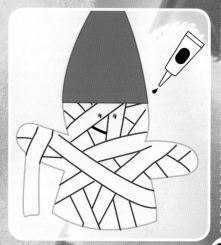

6 Cut the BOOTS from brown felt and glue them in place.

7 Cut out the BODY BACK from dark green felt and, using brown floss, sew to the back of the BODY. Leave a small opening.

8 Stuff the Mummy Gnome with a small amount of fiberfill, then close up the opening.

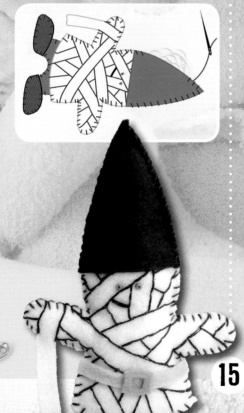

9 Cut the BELT from blue felt and glue to the BODY.

10 Cut the BUCKLE from light green felt and glue to the BELT.

MATERIALS

Green felt, gray felt, purple felt, white felt, yellow felt

Silver fabric

White stranded embroidery floss

2 green beads

2 silver sequins

3 sewing pins with black plastic heads

Toy fiberfill

Pins

Craft glue

Embroidery needle, Scissors

Templates from page 42

MAKING "ROBOT GNOME"

1 Photocopy or trace all the templates on page 42. Cut the HAT from green felt and the HEAD from gray felt. Glue the two together. Cut the BODY from purple felt and glue it to the bottom edge of the HEAD.

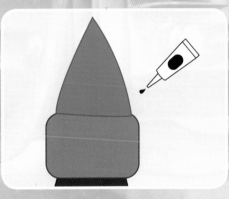

2 Cut the two LEG pieces from white felt and glue them to the bottom edge of the BODY.

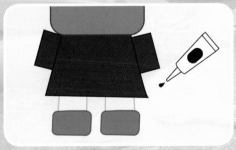

3 Cut the two FOOT pieces from green felt and glue them to the bottom of the LEGS.

4 Cut the two ARM pieces from purple felt and glue them to either side of the BODY.

ROBOT GNOME

He makes the coffee, cleans up, and loves watching *Glee*. His biggest fear is being banished to the backyard to rust. You wouldn't do that to him...would you?

5 Cut the BODY BACK from green felt. Cut the two EAR pieces from green felt and glue them to either side of the head.

6 To make each CLAW, glue some silver fabric to white felt. Cut out both CLAW templates from the silver and white. Glue each CLAW to the arm areas on the BODY BACK panel as shown.

7 Cut the EYE PLATE from white felt. Using white floss, sew a sequin and a bead to the end of the EYE PLATE.

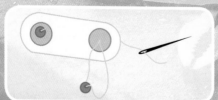

8 Sew the front of the robot to the BODY BACK using white floss, leaving a small opening.

9 Using a small amount of fiberfill, stuff the robot, making sure it gets into the point of the HAT, then close up the opening.

FEWER HUMANS, MORE ROBOTS!

10 Glue a piece of silver fabric to white felt and cut the BELT and BEARD from this. Cut the BUCKLE from yellow felt and glue the BUCKLE to the BELT.

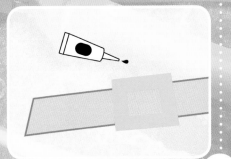

11 Glue the BELT, BEARD, and EYE PLATE in place.

12 Carefully push one of the pins into the very top of the HAT, allowing about ½ inch/1cm to protrude. Do the same on both ears, pushing the pin through the center of the felt and into the head.

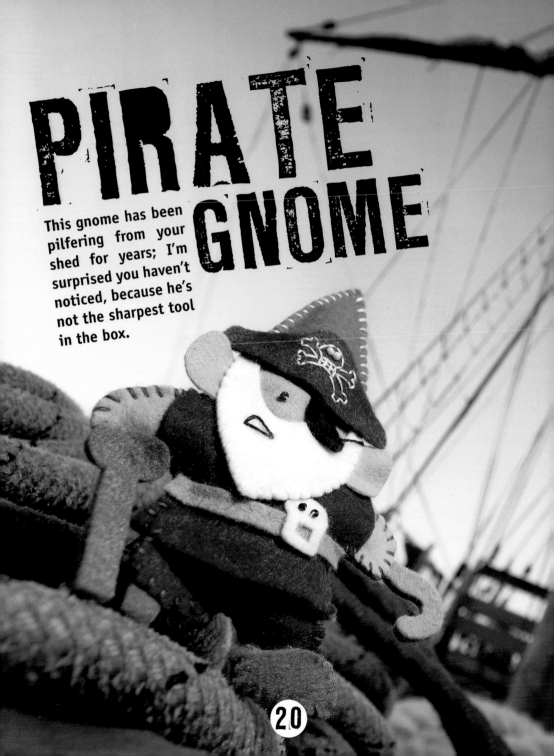

PIRATE GNOME

This gnome has been pilfering from your shed for years; I'm surprised you haven't noticed, because he's not the sharpest tool in the box.

MATERIALS

Dark green felt, light green felt,
peach felt, white felt, black felt,
dark blue felt, beige felt, brown felt
White, brown, and black stranded
embroidery floss
2 small white beads, 2 small black beads,
1 small blue bead, Toy fiberfill, Pins
Craft glue, Embroidery needle, Scissors
Templates from page 43

MAKING "PIRATE GNOME"

1 Photocopy or trace all the templates on page 43. Cut the HAT BRIM from dark green felt. Using white floss, sew the skull and crossbones emblem. Use the two small white beads to create the eyes on the skull. Cut the HAT from light green felt and then glue the HAT BRIM to the bottom edge of the HAT.

2 Cut the HEAD from peach felt and the BEARD from white felt. Glue the BEARD to the HEAD.

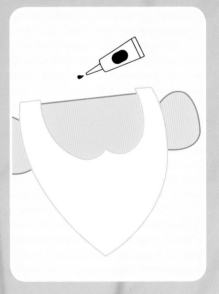

3 Glue the HAT to the top edge of the HEAD. Cut the EYE PATCH from black felt and glue to the HEAD. Use the black floss to create the tie for the EYE PATCH.

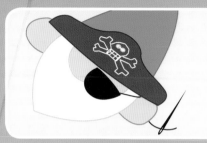

4 Now sew the mouth using black floss. Then, using white floss, sew on the small blue bead to create the eye.

5 Cut the HEAD BACK from light green felt and then sew to the back of the head with white floss. Leave a small opening. Stuff the head with a small amount of fiberfill, then close up the opening.

6 Cut the BODY from blue felt and the PANTS from dark green felt. Glue the PANTS to the bottom edge of the BODY. Cut the HANDS from peach felt and glue to the BODY. Cut the BOOT from the brown felt and glue to the long leg on the PANTS.

7 Cut the BODY BACK from brown felt and the HOOK from the beige felt. Glue the HOOK in position. Sew the BODY BACK to the back of the BODY with brown floss, leaving a small opening.

8 Stuff the BODY with a small amount of fiberfill, then close up the opening.

SHIVER ME TIMBERS!

11 Turn the BODY over and sew to the HEAD BACK using brown floss.

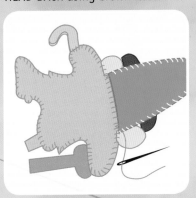

9 Cut the CRUTCH from brown felt and glue onto the RIGHT HAND.

12 Lift the BEARD and dab a small amount of glue to fix the BEARD to the BODY.

10 Cut the BUCKLE from white felt. Using white floss, sew the two black beads to the BUCKLE to create the eyes of a skull. Cut the BELT from beige felt and glue to the BODY. Glue the BUCKLE to the BELT.

MAKING "GARDEN GNOME"

1 Photocopy or trace all the templates on page 44. Cut out the FACE and NOSE from peach felt. Cut out the BEARD from white felt and glue the BEARD to the FACE. Glue the NOSE in place in the center of the FACE.

2 Cut the HAT from blue felt and glue the bottom edge to the top edge of the FACE. Sew the two eyes using black floss.

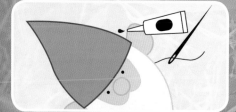

3 Cut the HEAD BACK from blue felt and sew to the back of the head. Use white floss to sew the BEARD and blue floss to do the HAT, leaving a small opening. Stuff the head with a small amount of fiberfill and then close up the opening.

MATERIALS

White felt, peach felt, blue felt, green felt, brown felt, gray felt, red felt, orange felt
Black, white, blue, and brown stranded embroidery floss, Toy fiberfill
1 large plastic-coated paper clip
1 small white bead
Pins, Craft glue, Embroidery needle, Scissors
Templates from page 44

GARDEN GNOME

The silent guard takes his job very seriously; he appears to be just your "friendly backyard gnome" but this front will help him eliminate all potential threats before you've even noticed anything is wrong.

4 Cut the BODY from green felt and the ARMS from peach felt. Glue the ARMS in place. Cut the PANTS from blue felt and glue to the bottom of the BODY.

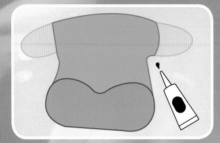

5 Cut the BODY BACK from green felt and sew to the BODY. Use white floss for the arms and green for the rest of the body, leaving a small opening. Stuff the body with fiberfill, then close up the opening.

6 Cut the BOOTS from brown felt and glue to the PANTS. Cut the BELT from gray felt and the BUCKLE from red felt. Glue the BUCKLE to the BELT and then glue the BELT to the BODY, tucking the ends under the tips of the BOOTS.

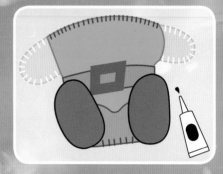

7 Turn the completed body and head pieces over and sew the two together, giving the head a slight tilt. Lift up the BEARD and dab a small amount of glue to fix the BEARD to the BODY.

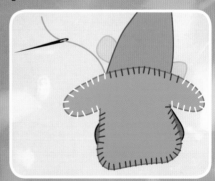

GNOMES
FOR LIFE!

8 Cut the two FISH from orange felt and stitch the detail to one of the FISH panels using brown floss.

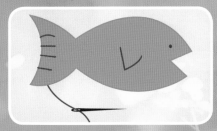

9 Straighten out the paper clip and then bend over one end about 1¼ inches/3cm down. Cut the two FISHING RODS from brown felt. Using a good blob of glue, sandwich the paperclip between the two FISHING RODS. Allow the glue to set.

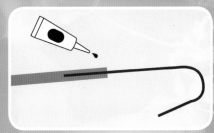

10 Cut the REEL from red felt. Using white floss, sew one line to create the handle arm on the REEL. Now sew the bead to the outside end of the handle arm to create the handle.

11 Sew the two FISHING ROD panels together with brown floss. Glue the REEL to the FISHING ROD. Glue the FISH to the end of the paper clip. Allow to dry.

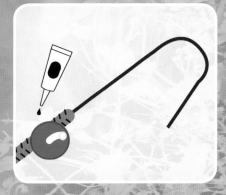

12 Sew the two FISH together, using brown floss. Sew the end of the FISHING ROD to the LEFT ARM and left-hand BOOT using brown floss.

BABY GNOME

This little fella is as cute as they come but watch out for those tantrums—he can be terribly *gnaughty* and that rattle can become a lethal weapon.

MATERIALS

Mauve felt, white felt, light pink felt,
green felt, blue felt, dark blue felt,
turquoise felt, red felt
White and green stranded embroidery floss
2 small blue beads
1 large dark green bead
Pins, Craft glue, Toy fiberfill
Embroidery needle, Scissors
Templates from page 45

MAKING "BABY GNOME"

1 Photocopy or trace all the templates
on page 45. Cut the HAT and HAT TOP
from mauve felt. Glue the HAT TOP to
the top edge of the HAT.

2 Cut the BEARD from white felt and
the FACE from light pink felt. Glue the
BEARD to the FACE. Glue the HAT to
the top of the HEAD.

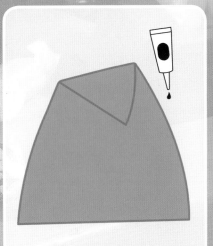

3 Cut the EYES from white felt. Using white floss, sew a bead to each of the EYES and then sew them to the FACE. Cut the PACIFIER from green felt. Sew the large bead to the PACIFIER and then to the BEARD with green floss.

4 Cut the HEAD BACK from mauve felt and sew to the back of the head with white floss. Leave a small opening. Stuff the head with a small amount of fiberfill, then close up the opening.

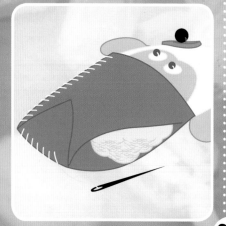

5 Cut the two BODY panels from light pink felt. Sew the two together with white floss, leaving a small opening. Stuff the BODY with a small amount of fiberfill, then close up the opening.

6 Cut the DIAPER from blue felt and glue to the BODY. Cut the BELT from turquoise felt and glue to the DIAPER. Cut the BUCKLE from red felt and glue to the BELT.

7 Turn the BODY over. Sew the BODY to the HEAD BACK using white floss.

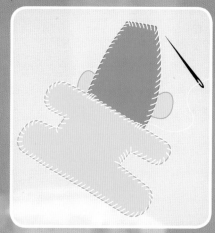

HE MAY GET RATTLED!

8 Lift the BEARD and dab a small amount of glue to fix the BEARD to the BODY.

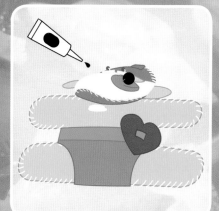

9 Cut the RATTLE from the dark blue felt and the RATTLE PANELS from turquoise felt. Glue the RATTLE PANELS onto the RATTLE.

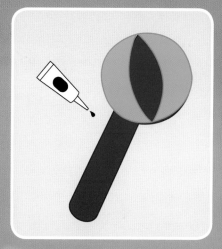

10 Glue the RATTLE onto the right hand and foot.

MAKING "NINJA GNOME"

1 Photocopy or trace all the templates on page 46. Cut the FACE from peach felt and the BEARD from white felt. Glue the BEARD to the FACE.

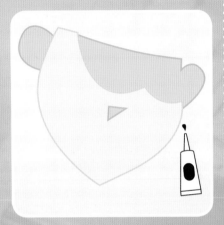

2 Cut the HAT from red felt and glue to the top edge of the FACE. Sew in the eyes with black floss.

MATERIALS

Peach felt, white felt, red felt, black felt, gray felt

Black, red, white, and gray stranded embroidery floss

Toy fiberfill

Pins

Craft glue

Embroidery needle

Scissors

Templates from page 46

NINJA GNOME

This gnome was once thought to be the best protection. But this crazy, fighting, ninja gnome revels in havoc and will steal your worldly possessions just for something to do.

3 Cut the HEAD BACK from red felt and stitch to the back of the head. Use white floss to sew the BEARD and red floss to do the HAT, leaving a small opening. Stuff the head with a small amount of fiberfill and then close up the opening.

4 Cut the BODY and PANTS from black felt and glue together. Cut the SHOES from red felt and glue to the bottom of the PANTS.

5 Cut the HANDS from peach felt and glue to the BODY.

6 Cut the BODY BACK from black felt and sew to the back of the body with black floss, leaving a small opening. Stuff the body with a small amount of toy fiberfill and then close up the opening.

7 Cut the BELT from red felt and glue to the BODY.

8 Cut the BUCKLE from white felt and glue to the BELT.

9 Turn the body over and stitch the HEAD BACK to the BODY BACK using black floss.

10 Cut the SWORD pieces from gray felt and glue them together.

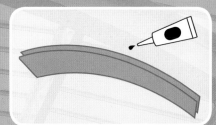

NINJA IN TRAINING!

11 Sew the small end of the SWORD to the LEFT HAND using gray floss. Cut the HILT from black felt and glue over the end of the SWORD, covering the stitching.

SK8R
GNOME

He will make ramps out of your garden ornaments, nosegrind along your deck and use your pond

MATERIALS

White felt, light pink felt, red felt, green felt, black felt, brown felt, yellow felt, blue felt

Black, white, light pink, green, and red stranded embroidery floss

4 wooden beads

Toy fiberfill, Pins, Craft glue, Embroidery needle, Scissors

Templates from page 47

MAKING "SK8R GNOME"

1 Photocopy or trace all the templates on page 47. Cut the BEARD from white felt and the FACE from light pink felt. Glue the two together. Using black floss, sew the two eyes.

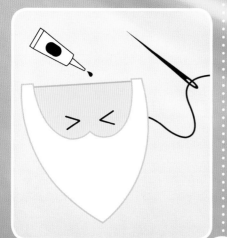

2 Cut the CAP PEAK from red felt and glue to the right-hand top edge of the FACE. Cut the HAT from red felt and glue to the top edge of the FACE.

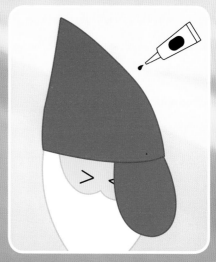

3 Cut the HEAD BACK from red felt and sew to the back of the head. Use white floss to sew the BEARD and red floss for the HAT, leaving a small opening. Stuff with a small amount of fiberfill and then close up the opening.

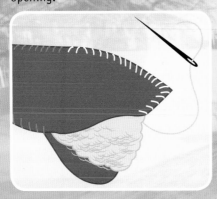

5 Cut the BODY BACK from green felt and position on the back of the body. Sew the ARMS to the BODY BACK with light pink floss. Sew the rest of the body together with green floss, leaving an opening at the top. Stuff the body with a small amount of fiberfill and then close up the opening.

4 Cut the BODY from green felt and the PANTS from black felt. Glue the two together. Cut the SHOES from brown felt and glue to the bottom of the PANTS. Cut the two ARMS from light pink felt and glue to the back of the BODY.

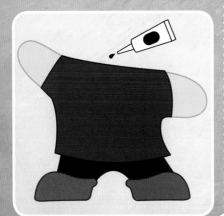

6 Cut the FINGERS from light pink felt and glue to the end of the RIGHT ARM.

7 Turn the body over and sew the HEAD BACK to the body using green floss.

10 Cut the SKATEBOARD from blue felt and the AXLES from brown felt. Glue the AXLES in position. Sew the four wooden beads to either side of the AXLES using white floss.

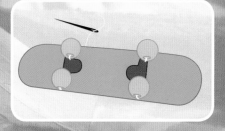

8 Put a dab of glue under the BEARD on the BODY to hold the head down at the front.

9 Cut the BELT from brown felt and glue onto the BODY. Cut the BUCKLE from yellow felt and glue to the BELT.

11 Glue the SKATEBOARD to the left SHOE and the LEFT ARM.

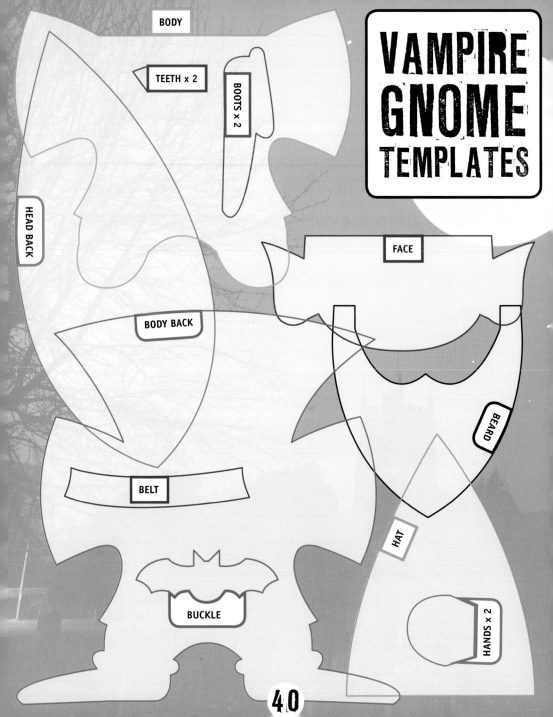

BODY

TEETH x 2

BOOTS x 2

VAMPIRE
GNOME
TEMPLATES

HEAD BACK

FACE

BODY BACK

BEARD

BELT

HAT

BUCKLE

HANDS x 2

40

MUMMY GNOME TEMPLATES

HAT

BOOTS x 2

BELT

PANTS

BODY BACK

BUCKLE

BODY

41

ROBOT GNOME TEMPLATES

EYE PLATE

BODY BACK

HAT

FOOT x 2

CLAW x 2

BUCKLE

BELT

ARM x 2

HEAD

BODY

EAR x 2

LEG x 2

BEARD

PIRATE GNOME TEMPLATES

HAT BRIM

PANTS

HEAD BACK

CRUTCH

BEARD

EYE PATCH

BELT

RIGHT HAND

LEFT HAND

HEAD

BODY BACK

HAT

BOOT

BODY

HOOK

BUCKLE

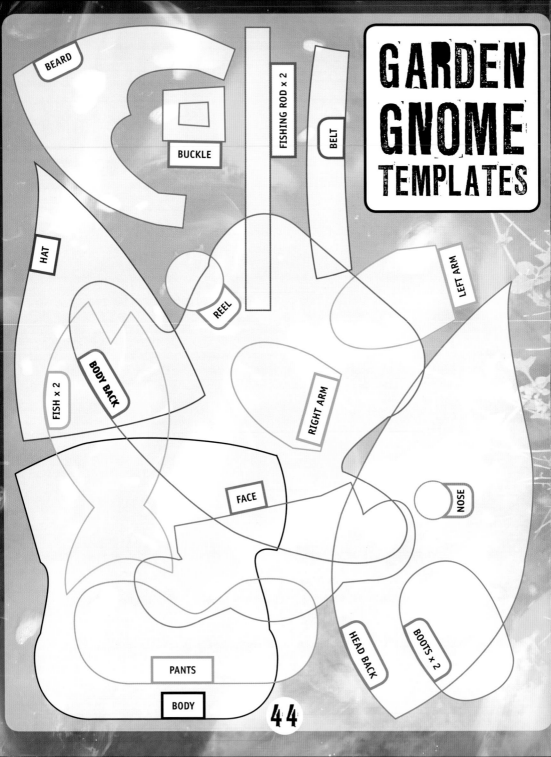

GARDEN GNOME TEMPLATES

BEARD

BUCKLE

FISHING ROD x 2

BELT

HAT

REEL

LEFT ARM

FISH x 2

BODY BACK

RIGHT ARM

FACE

NOSE

PANTS

HEAD BACK

BOOTS x 2

BODY

HEAD BACK

RATTLE PANEL x 2

BEARD

BABY GNOME TEMPLATES

HAT

FACE

EYES x 2

DIAPER

BELT

BODY x 2

BUCKLE

RATTLE

PACIFIER

HAT TOP

45

NINJA GNOME TEMPLATES

BELT

HAT

SWORD x 2

HEAD BACK

RIGHT SHOE

RIGHT HAND

LEFT HAND

BEARD

BODY BACK

BUCKLE

LEFT SHOE

FACE

BODY

HILT

PANTS

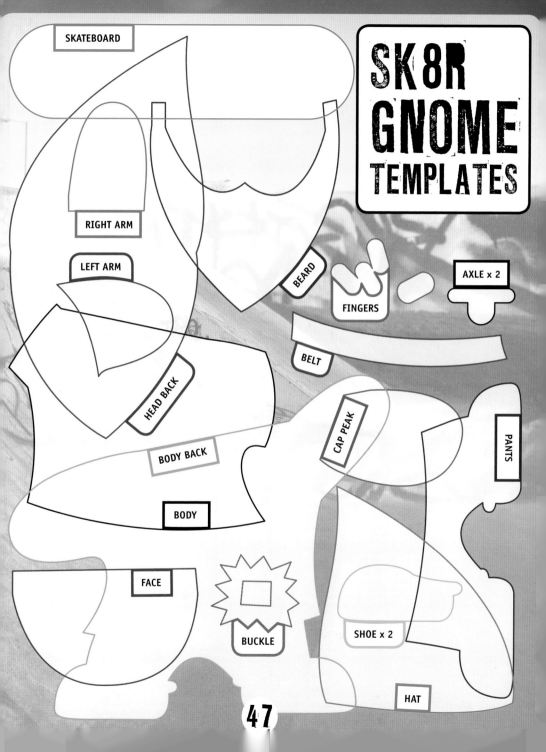

SKATEBOARD

SK8R GNOME TEMPLATES

RIGHT ARM

LEFT ARM

BEARD

FINGERS

AXLE x 2

BELT

HEAD BACK

BODY BACK

CAP PEAK

PANTS

BODY

FACE

BUCKLE

SHOE x 2

HAT